AF560280
WHEELS AND WONDERS
INVENTIONS AND CREATIONS
MOONSTONE

Published in Moonstone
by Rupa Publications India Pvt. Ltd 2024
7/16, Ansari Road, Daryaganj
New Delhi 110002

Sales centres:
Bengaluru Chennai
Hyderabad Jaipur Kathmandu
Kolkata Mumbai Prayagraj

P-ISBN: 978-93-90260-69-0
E-ISBN: 978-93-90260-62-1

First impression 2024

10 9 8 7 6 5 4 3 2 1

Printed in India

CONTENTS

TRANSPORTATION

CONTENTS

WONDERS OF THE WORLD

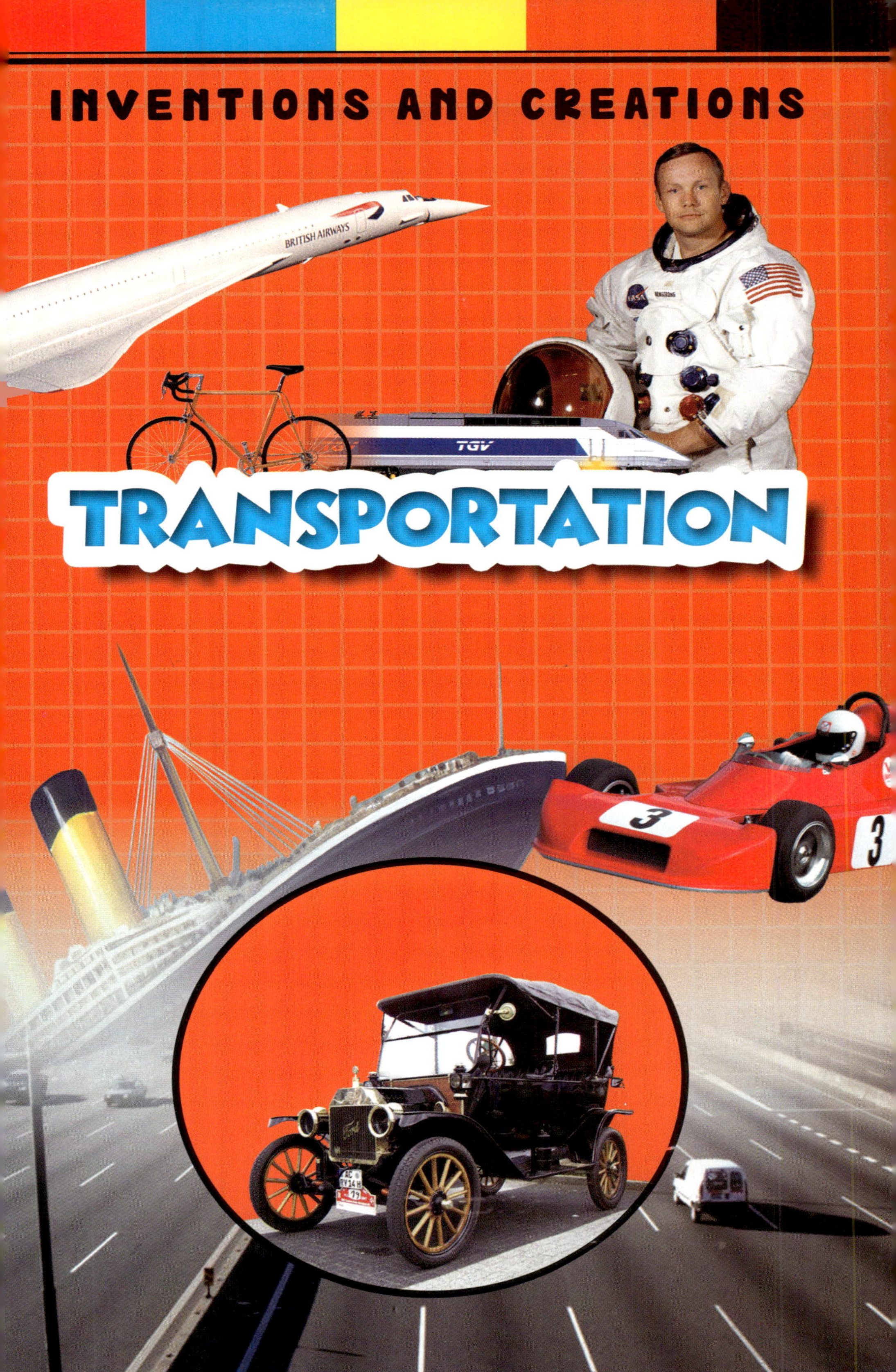
INVENTIONS AND CREATIONS
BRITISH AIRWAYS
TGV
TRANSPORTATION
3
3

Introduction

Transportation involves moving people or goods from one place to another using various modes. Transportation has been regarded as the foundation of civilizations and trade between them. Without transportation, no exchange of communication, culture or trade would be possible.

Land, water, and air are the three main modes of transportation. Vehicles with wheels, such as cars, trains, and metro rails, are means of land transport; boats and ships are means of water transport; and aeroplanes are means of air transport. Some means of transport are engine-powered, while others are engineless. Engine-powered vehicles run on petrol, diesel, CNG (compressed natural gas), or gas turbines (in jet engines). With the growing concern to combat pollution caused by vehicles, scientists are developing vehicles that would solely run on environmentally friendly sources of energy.

Early Modes of Transportation

Thousands of years ago, people used simple things to transport goods. For example, they often carried items on their backs. As time moved on, people began to use animals, sleds and wood logs to transfer items and goods from one place to another.

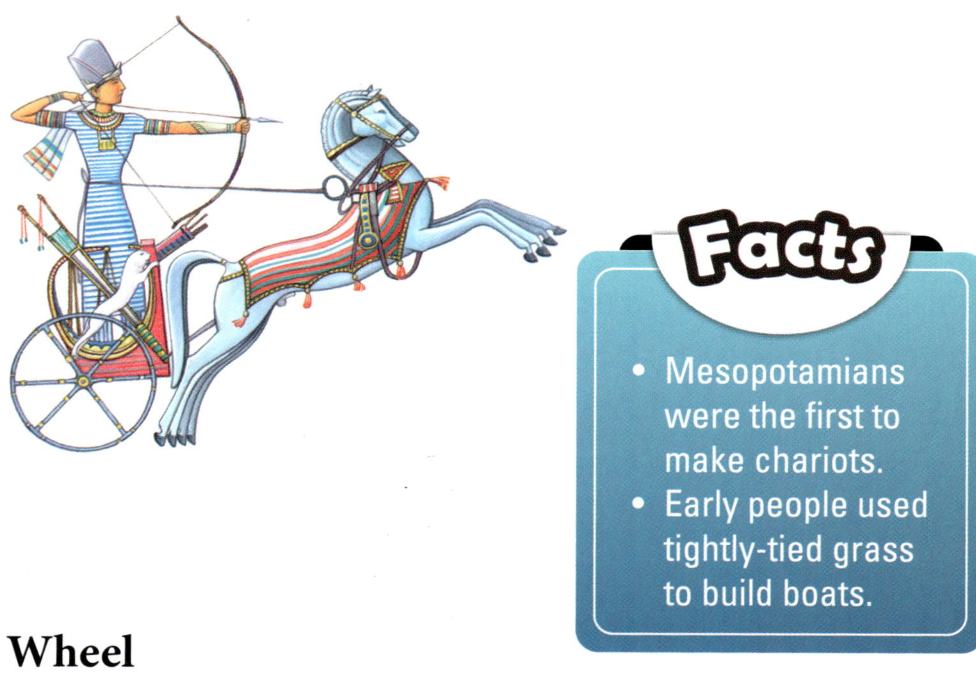

Facts

- Mesopotamians were the first to make chariots.
- Early people used tightly-tied grass to build boats.

Wheel

A wheel is a circular disc that revolves around a central axis. The first wheels were made of solid wood. They were made by cutting circular slices from tree trunks. Wheels were invented around 3,500 BC in Mesopotamia. The Mesopotamians used wheels to move their chariots.

Travois

A travois was a device used by Native Americans to carry goods and food. It was made of two long crossed poles tied to the sides of a dog or a horse. The rear portion had a netted hoop or ladder of crossed sticks on which the goods were placed.

Animal

Animals were the earliest mode of transportation. Humans tamed animals like horses, dogs, deer, camels and mules. These animals were used to carry humans and loads from one place to another. Later, the animals were attached to carts or sleds for carrying humans and goods.

When was wheel invented and where?

Bicycle

Bicycles are human-powered, two-wheeled vehicles. The rider sits on the seat and uses the handles to control its direction. In many places, it is an important mode of transport, especially in developing countries like China, Brazil and India.

First Bicycle

The world's first bicycle was made from wood. It was designed in France by Comte de Sivrac in the 1790s. It had no pedals, so it had to be dragged along. It also had no handlebars, so it would only go straight.

Kinds of Bicycles

There are several types of bicycles, each with its own unique features. Usually, there are five kinds of bicycles: road, mountain, hybrid, juvenile and specialty.

Eden for Cyclists

The Netherlands is the "Eden for cyclists." It has a population of 17 million. Of this, about 12 million people own bicycles. People go to their offices and schools on bicycles. The Netherlands has a separate lane, special traffic lights and signs for cyclists.

Le Tour de France

Le Tour de France is the biggest cycling competition in the world. It started in 1903 and since then, it is held every year in France. During the event, around 200 riders ride all over France and cover a total distance of 3,500 kilometers (about 2,175 miles). The competition lasts for three weeks and is watched by about four million television viewers in 170 different countries.

- Air-filled tires were first used on bicycles and not on motorcars.
- American Olympic Cyclist John Howard once rode a bicycle at the speed of 245 kilometers per hour (about 152 miles per hour).

Who designed the first bicycle?

Motorcycle

Motorcycles are two- or three-wheeled motor vehicles. They are powered by gasoline engines. They have two seats and sometimes a sidecar for a third person. They include scooters, mopeds and mini bikes.

First Motorcycle

The first motorcycle was invented in 1869 by Sylvester Howard Roper, an American, and had a steam engine. The first gasoline-powered motorcycle was built in 1885 by Gottlieb Daimler, a German engineer.

Harley-Davidson

In 1903, two Americans, Arthur Davidson and William Harley, built the first Harley-Davidson motorcycle. Their motorcycles are popularly known as Harleys. In 1909, they introduced V-twin engine technology for the first time. This engine gave a deep, rumbling sound, which made Harleys famous all over the world.

Moped

Mopeds are lightweight motorbikes. They have a motor and two pedals, which are used to start them. They are powered by a low-power gasoline engine. Mopeds were invented in the 1950s and are known all over the world by different names.

Scooter

Scooters are two-wheeled vehicles meant to carry two people. They have a low-power gasoline engine, which is fitted above the rear wheel. Scooters are heavier than mopeds and lighter than motorcycles. The first scooter was the Vespa, which was built in 1946 in Italy by Piaggio and Company.

Facts

- The first gasoline-powered motorcycle was made from a wooden bicycle.
- The first scooters were able to move at a speed of 75 kilometres per hour (about 47 miles per hour).
- Trikes are motorcycles that move on three wheels.

Who invented the first motorcycle and when?

Automobile

Automobiles are vehicles with wheels that are powered by an internal combustion engine. Different types of automobiles include cars, vans, buses, and trucks. Cars, buses, and vans are used for transporting people and passengers.

First Four-Wheeled Car

The world's first workable four-wheeled car was designed in Germany in 1886. It was built by Gottlieb Daimler and Wilhelm Maybach. The car was a horseless carriage powered by a lightweight, high-speed gasoline engine. It was known as the motorwagen.

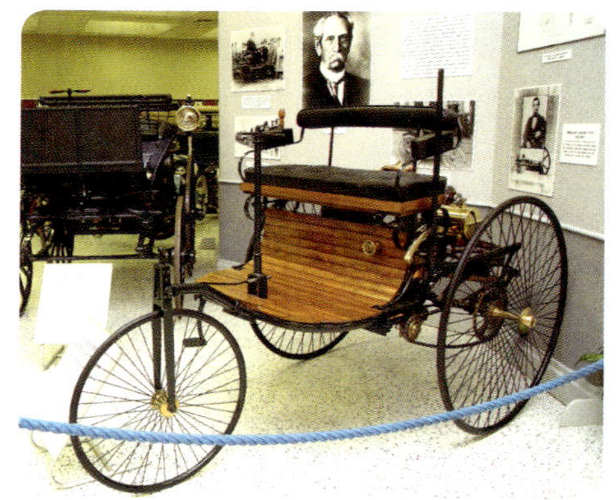

First Jeep

Jeeps are powerful, four-wheeled, open automobiles. They were built for the first time during World War II. They were built for the United States Army to travel through muddy and hilly terrain. They could carry six people and move at a speed of 105 kilometres per hour (about 65 miles per hour).

Henry Ford

Henry Ford is known as the father of the modern assembly line. An assembly line is used in mass production. Henry Ford started making Ford Model T cars using assembly lines. The first Model T car was built in 1908 and cost $950. However, once assembly line production was implemented, the cost was reduced to $440.

First Grand Prix

The Grand Prix is a car-racing competition held on closed highways or roads. The first Grand Prix was held in France in 1906. It was named the Grand Prix de Pau. Only 32 participants from 12 car companies took part in the race. They covered a distance of 1,260 kilometers (about 783 miles).

Facts

- Maybach is a luxury car named after Wilhelm Maybach.
- Jeep was popularly called "peep" as a short form of general-purpose vehicle.
- The Grand Prix is now popularly known as F1 or Formula 1 racing.

? The first Model T car was built in ______.

Bus And Truck

Buses and trucks are heavy vehicles. Buses carry passengers, and trucks carry bulky goods. Both buses and trucks have powerful engines and sturdy bodies. They are powered by diesel, liquefied petroleum gas (LPG), or compressed natural gas (CNG).

Mobile Library

Mobile libraries are libraries on wheels. Mobile libraries provide books to people living in villages and remote areas who do not have easy access to libraries. The first mobile library was made in the 1850s on a horse-drawn carriage.

Invention of the Truck

The world's first truck, Daimler-Motoren-Gesellschaft, was built in 1896. It was powered by a gasoline engine and built by Gottlieb Daimler. He built trucks to transport heavy cargo from one place to another by road.

Broadcast Van

Broadcast vans are TV or radio broadcasting vehicles. The British Broadcasting Corporation used a broadcast van to cover the coronation of King George VI and Elizabeth in 1937. This was the first use of a broadcast van in history.

- The world's longest truck was 1,474.3 metres (about 4,837 feet).
- The first motorised mobile library was introduced in 1912.
- The word "bus" is a short form of "omnibus," meaning "for everyone."
- "Truck" in Greek means "heavy wheel."

Routemaster

Routemasters are red-coloured double-decker buses. They were introduced in London in 1956 to replace trolleybuses. They were a part of London city public transport until 2005.

Gottlieb Daimler built first gasoline powered engine. True or False

Watercraft

Watercrafts are vehicles designed to travel on water. Early watercraft were powered by wind and steam. Today, diesel and jet engines power watercraft. Watercraft are used for commerce, military missions, and pleasure as well.

Dugout

Dugouts are the oldest boats or canoes. They are lightweight boats with round ends. They were made of hollowed tree trunks. The earliest known dugouts were made around 6,000 BC. They were used by the Dutch and American Indians.

Aircraft Carrier

Aircraft carriers are large warships used as floating airbases. They are used for the takeoff and landing of military aircraft. Aircraft carriers were used for the first time during World War I. The British ship, HMS Furious, was one of the first aircraft carriers. It was a cruise ship that was converted into an aircraft carrier. Its wooden deck was used as an airstrip for fighter planes.

Titanic

The Titanic was the largest luxury ship in the world. A steam engine powered it. People believed that the Titanic was unsinkable. However, on its maiden voyage, it struck an iceberg in the Atlantic (on April 14, 1912) and sank. Out of the 2,220 people aboard, about 1,500 died.

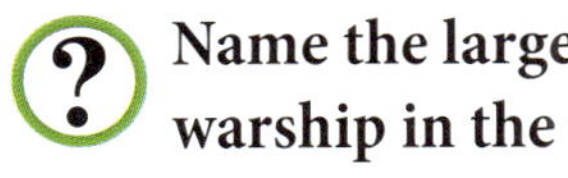

Name the largest warship in the world.

- The first lifeboat was tested in 1790 by two Englishmen, William Wouldhave and Lionel Lukin.
- The largest supertanker is as long as the Sears Tower.
- The USS Gerald R. Ford, the US Navy's newest supercarrier, is the largest warship in the world.
- The Titanic was the first ship to have a heated swimming pool.

Train

Trains are a series of cars moved by locomotives. They move on two parallel lines known as rails. Rails are made of steel. They carry goods and passengers. Trains can be moved by steam, diesel or electric engines.

George Stephenson

George Stephenson was an English railway engineer. In 1814, he built the world's first successful steam engine—the Blucher. The Blucher could pull 30 tonnes of freight and move at a speed of six kilometres (about 4 miles).

TGV

TGVs are high-speed electric trains. They run on special high-speed rail tracks. The first TGV ran in France in 1981, between Paris and Lyon. TGVs are the world's fastest wheel trains and can cover a distance of 575 kilometres (357.28 miles) in an hour.

Maglev

Maglevs are high-speed trains that move on special tracks known as guideways. These trains do not touch the track but float above it. Japan and Germany are two leaders in Maglev technology. Maglev trains can ride at a speed of 450 kilometres per hour (about 280 miles per hour).

Longest Train Journey

The Trans-Siberian Line is the longest railway line in the world. It covers a distance of 10,214 kilometres (about 6,128 miles) from Moscow to Vladivostok. The total train journey takes around six days.

- Maglev trains do not have wheels.
- The world's longest train is the BHP Iron Ore, which is 7.352 km (4.568 miles) long.

Name the longest railway line in the world?

Aeroplane

Aeroplanes are heavier-than-air aircraft with fixed wings. They are powered by propellers or jet engines. Early aeroplanes flew at low speeds. Modern aeroplanes can now fly faster than the speed of sound.

Wright Brothers

The first successful aeroplane was built by the American brothers Wilbur and Orville Wright. In 1903, they made the first flight in history at Kitty Hawk, in North Carolina (United States). The first flight lasted for just 12 seconds and covered a distance of about 36.5 metres (about 119 feet).

Concorde

The Concorde was the first supersonic aeroplane. Supersonic planes are able to fly at twice the speed of sound. It was first flown in 1969. The first commercial flight of the Concorde was between Paris and London in 1976. Concordes were in service until 2003. The last flight occurred on November 26, 2003.

Largest Passenger Airplane

The Airbus A380 is the largest passenger aeroplane in the world. It is a 73-metre (about 240 feet)-long double-decker plane. The super jumbo can typically seat 525 passengers but is designed to carry as many as 853 passengers. Singapore Airlines took the first commercial flight of the Airbus A380 on October 25, 2007, from Singapore to Sydney.

- The Ukrainian-built An-225 Mriya (Cossack) is the biggest aeroplane in the world.
- The Chinese were the first to develop the concept of a helicopter.
- The first permanent airport for commercial purposes was built in Königsberg, East Prussia, in 1922.

________ is the largest passenger aeroplane in the world.

Military Aircraft

Military aircraft are used in military operations or warfare. Some aircraft carry armies, goods, and weapons to the battlefield or airbase. Others, like fighter planes, fly on spy missions or are used for air attacks.

The Beginning

The Italians used military aeroplanes for the first time in 1911 against the Turks. However, aeroplanes were more popularly used for the first time during World War I. They were known as fighting scouts and were used to spy on and bomb enemy positions.

Airship

Airships are large floating aircraft. They are filled with lighter-than-air gases such as hydrogen and helium. Airships have diesel engines to drive them in the right direction. The first airship was called the Zeppelin. Germans used Zeppelins during World War I (1914–18) as bombers and spy planes.

First Jet Engine

The Messerschmitt Me 262, also known as the Turbo or the Stormbird, was the first aeroplane to use a jet engine. The Germans used this fighter plane during World War II. It was the world's fastest fighter plane at the time.

Facts

- The Zeppelin airship was named after its inventor, Ferdinand von Zeppelin.
- The first letter in the name of fighter planes indicates the type of plane.
- For example, F in F-16 means fighter planes and B in B-2 means bomber.

? **What was a zeppelin?**

Submarine and Hovercraft

Submarines and hovercrafts are special types of watercraft. Submarines move underwater, while hovercrafts move above the surface of water. A submarine looks like a big fish and can move swiftly under the deep sea. Hovercrafts are also called amphibious vehicles as they can move both on land and in water.

How do submarines dive and float?

Submarines are made of two hulls or shells. The space between the two hulls, is known as the ballast tank. For diving, this tank is filled with water, which makes the submarine heavy enough to sink. To make the submarine float on the surface of water, compressed air is filled in the tank to push water out. This makes the submarine lighter to float.

Hovercraft

Hovercrafts are special vehicles that move on cushions of air. The air pressure produces a 0.25-centimetre-thick cushion, which makes it hover on the surface. The first hovercraft travelled across the English Channel in 1959.

Submersible Craft

Submersible crafts are underwater vehicles like submarines. They are shorter than submarines and have cameras and movable arms. Submersible crafts are used for underwater tasks, like exploring shipwreck remains and repairing oil rigs and submarines.

- Submarines have periscopes to see above the water.
- The new models of hovercrafts can cross the English Channel in just 20 minutes.
- The Typhoon Class (Soviet and Russian) is the largest submarine in the world.

Vehicles that can travel both over land and water are called _______.

Space Flight

Space flights are journeys made into outer space. Outer space is the empty region of the universe outside the Earth's atmosphere. Space shuttles and spacecraft are special vehicles that carry humans, animals, and machines into space.

First Spaceflight

The former Soviet Union launched the world's first artificial or man-made satellite, Sputnik, into space on October 4, 1957. Artificial satellites orbit the earth and are used to study the universe, forecast weather, and transmit telephone calls.

First Human to Fly into Space

Yuri Gagarin was the first human to fly into space. Gagarin was a Soviet cosmonaut. On April 12, 1961, Yuri Gagarin flew on the space shuttle Vostok I. He also became the first human to orbit the Earth.

First Human on the Moon

In July 1969, Neil Armstrong became the first human to step on the moon. Neil Armstrong was followed by Edwin "Buzz" Aldrin. They were American astronauts and flew on the Apollo 11 space mission. They stayed on the moon for two and a half hours.

International Space Station

The International Space Station (ISS) is a research laboratory built to perform experiments in space. Scientists from all over the world live and work here. They perform research in different fields of science, technology and medicine. The ISS is the largest structure ever built in space.

Facts

- A dog named "Laika" was the first living being to go into space.
- The flight of Yuri Gagarin lasted for 108 minutes.
- Skylab was the first American space station and Salyut 1 was the first Russian space station.

Who was the first person to travel into space?

Snow Vehicles

Many places around the world experience heavy snow in winter, while there are some places that remain covered in snow all year round. In such places, common modes of land transport cannot be used. People living in such places use special snow vehicles. Some are used to travel, while there are some specialised vehicles that are used to remove snow and clear roads.

Snow coach

A snow coach is like a bus that can travel in covered areas. It is equipped with large tyres and tracks. Snow coaches are multi-passenger vehicles. They can carry more than 20 people at a time.

Snowmobile

Snowmobiles are special vehicles that are used in snowy regions. These vehicles use skis instead of wheels and run on powerful gasoline engines. In 1958, Joseph Bombardier designed the snowmobiles. Bombardier invented snowmobiles for easy transportation on snow.

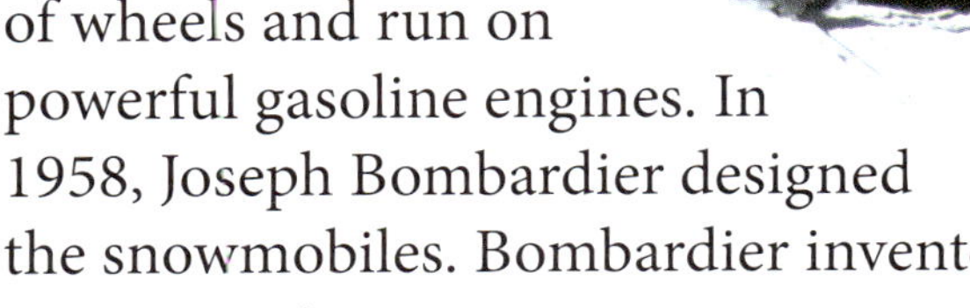

Snow Removal Vehicle

Snow removal vehicles are used to remove ice and snow from roads and restore the roads for travelers. There are different types of snow removal vehicles. Some are used to de-ice a place; some are used to remove snow, especially from sidewalks and parking lots; and some are used to smooth and level the snow.

- Dog sleds are a popular means of transport used to travel over ice and through snow.
- A snowplough is a snow removal device that is used for removing snow.

Who designed snowmobiles?

Special Transport

Some vehicles have additional machines or features that make them special, such as a fire engine or an ambulance.

Ambulance

Ambulances are special vehicles used to carry sick people. Sick or injured people are carried to hospitals from their homes or the place of the accident. The word "ambulance" means "to walk" or "move about." The first ambulance was used in France to carry injured soldiers from the battlefield in 1792.

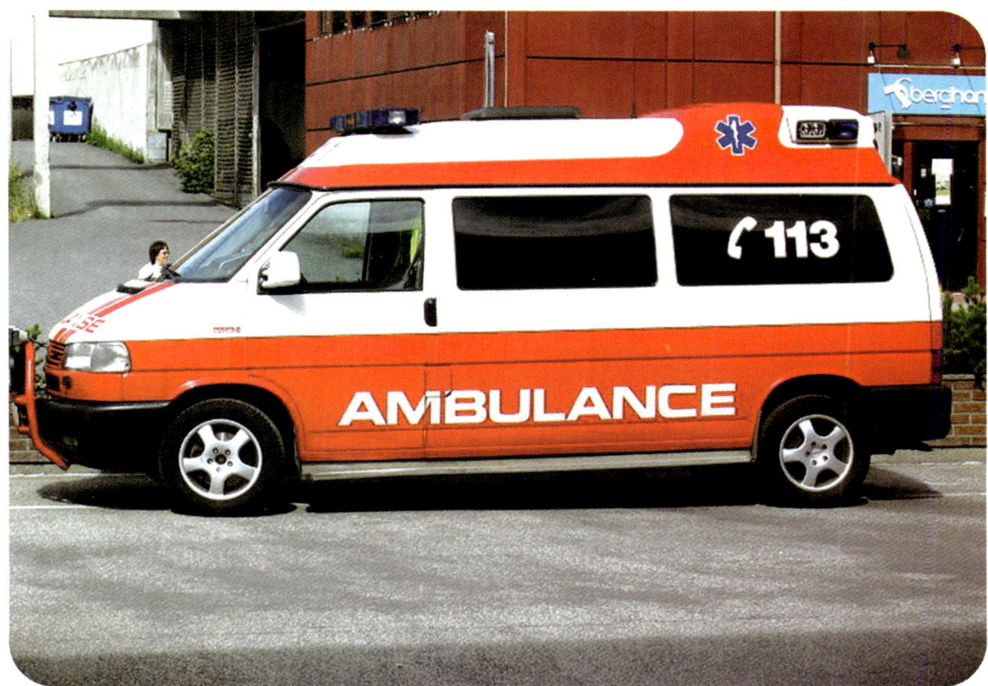

Tractor

Tractors are heavy-duty vehicles. Generally, tractors are used to pull or push heavy loads in agriculture, building and road construction sites, railway freight stations, and docks. John Froehlich, an American blacksmith, was the one to build the first tractor in 1892.

- The word "ambulance" on an ambulance is written in reverse letters for clear visibility in the rearview mirrors of vehicles ahead.
- The first military tank was built on the design of a tractor.
- Fire brigade pumps release around 2,800 litres (about 740 gallons) of water in one minute.

Fire Engines

Fire engines are vehicles used to extinguish fires. They are equipped with fire-fighting gear like water, extendable ladders and special clothing. The ladders can usually extend above 30 metres (about 98 feet).

What does the word 'ambulance' mean?

Traffic Control

Traffic control is a system of controlling traffic using signs, traffic lights and other devices. Traffic control is used to control traffic on the road, air, rail and water. Traffic control ensures the safe movements of pedestrians and vehicles. It also prevents accidents.

Traffic Sign

Traffic signs are special signs used to make traffic move in an orderly way. They are used on roads and highways. All traffic signs have different shapes, sizes, and colours. However, they are the same all over the world. They depict different road situations and display warnings.

No Right Turn

STOP

No Automobiles

Work Ahead

- English is an international language for traffic signals.
- Traffic lights all over the world follow Garrett's model.
- In the United States, there are more than 55 million traffic signs on the roads.

Traffic Light

Traffic lights worldwide have three colours: red, green, and yellow. Red is the colour of danger. It is used as a stop sign. Green reflects a refreshing nature. It is used to tell people to move on. Yellow stands out among red and green and cautions people to get ready to move or to stop.

First Traffic Lights

The first traffic lights were installed in London. They were installed at the intersection of George and Bridge Streets in 1868. The traffic lights had only red and green colours. The lights were powered by gas; however, modern traffic lights are powered by electricity or solar energy. The credit for inventing the first electric traffic light goes to Lester Wire of the United States. He invented electric traffic lights in 1912.

________ invented the first electric traffic light in 1912.

Boarding and Travelling

Pan-American Highway

The Pan-American Highway is the world's longest "drivable road." It is 48,000 kilometres (about 29,825 miles) long. It runs from Alaska to Chile and connects the continents of North America and South America.

King Fahd Airport

Dammam King Fahd International Airport in Saudi Arabia is the largest airport in the world in terms of land area. It covers an area of 780 square kilometres (301 square miles). The airport was opened for commercial aviation in November 1999. The passenger terminal of the airport has six stories and covers a total area of 327,000 square metres (3,519,798 square feet). The airport has a huge duty-free shopping area, a mosque, and a Royal Terminal. The Royal Terminal is reserved for the royal family of Saudi Arabia, government personnel, and official guests. The air cargo building is a two-story building constructed on an area of 39,500 square metres (425,174 square feet).

Grand Central Station

The Grand Central Station in New York City is the world's largest railway station in terms of platforms. It has 44 underground platforms on two levels. Grand Central Station was opened on February 2, 1913, and is the busiest railway station in the United States.

Rotterdam Port

The Rotterdam Port is the largest man-made port in the world. It was built in the 14th century in the Netherlands. Rotterdam Port is an important port in Europe for transferring cargo shipments. Every year, the port handles around 375 million metric tonnes of cargo.

Facts

- The cost of building the Channel Tunnel is equal to the cost of building 700 Golden Gate Bridges.
- Kansai International Airport in Japan is built over a sea.
- The Pan-American Highway passes through 14 countries.

How long is Pan-American Highway?

Road Train

Road trains are long and heavy vehicles that are used for the transportation of cargo in remote and rural areas. They are called road trains because they pull two or more trailers. These vehicles are largely used in Australia, Mexico, Argentina, Canada, and the United States.

Driving Road Trains

Professional drivers are required to drive and control road trains. The drivers have to be very careful and vigilant while driving these vehicles, as road trains can be over 50 metres long and weigh up to 200 tonnes. So the driver must not try to overtake other vehicles. He should drive at a prescribed speed limit, as it can become hard to stop or turn the vehicle instantly.

Name Game

In Canada, road trains are called Longer Combination Vehicles (LCVs) or Extended Length Vehicles (ELVs). The term 'road train' is frequently used in Australia.

Uses of Road Trains

Road trains are used for transporting livestock, goods, fuel, mineral ores, etc. These vehicles connect rural areas to urban areas, and many communities rely on their services. So, road trains help in the economic development of rural areas. These vehicles are cost-effective because they are fuel-efficient.

- Airport baggage trains and amusement park trains are trackless trains that transfer people from one place to another.
- Australia has the largest number for road trains in the world.
- The credit of inventing the modern road train goes to Kurt Johannsen.

Are road trains heavy vehicles?

Dump Truck

The dump truck is a large truck designed to transport materials to and from the construction site. They are also called dumper trucks. These trucks have a dumper attached to the back, and the dumper lifts contents from the truck to be deposited at the site.

Uses of Dump Trucks

Dump trucks are used for various purposes, such as collecting waste from houses, collecting material from construction sites, and transferring debris. Some dump trucks have lights that flash when their dumper is full.

Super Dump Truck

A super dump truck is a truck with a trailing axle and a load-bearing axle. The trailing axle can lift up to 13,000 pounds of load. The axle trails 11 to 13 feet behind the truck body. The trailing axle uses its two powered arms to clear off the load. These dump trucks can carry more load as compared to other dump trucks. This is why they are called super dump trucks.

Types of Dump Trucks

Dump trucks are of various types to carry different materials. A standard dump truck is usually a six- or ten-wheeler. The truck's dump body is attached to the frame. A transfer dump truck is a standard dump truck that pulls a separate trailer. It is used to carry gravel, dirt, sand, or other construction material. On the other hand, a site dump truck has two axle trailers pulled by a tractor. They are capable of quickly loading materials.

- Robert T. Mawhinney made the first dump truck in 1920. He attached a dump box to a flatbed truck.
- Dump trucks are also called production trucks.
- Super dump trucks can carry 26 tonnes of loads at a time.

Who made the first dump truck?

Animal Transport Vehicles

Animal transport vehicles are used for transporting animals from one place to another. These vehicles are specially designed to carry animals such as horses, livestock, etc. These vehicles have separate driver cabins and animal chambers.

Animal Transport Vans

Animal transport vans carry animals in separate cages and transport them for shorter distances. The vehicle has a temperature and moisture control unit and a ventilation system. The free flow of air is important to remove the foul smell of animal urine and dung.

Facts

- Transporting animals on hoofs for shorter distances is still popular among animal farmers.
- Chassis-mount is an animal transportation vehicle and can be built of any size chassis.

Horse Trailer

Horse trailers are used for carrying horses. Some are built for carrying only two or three horses, while others can carry six to eight horses. These trailers need trucks to pull them. However, some horse trailers are large enough to carry a significant number of animals and need semi-trailers to haul them. Horse trailers are designed to provide a smooth, comfortable, and safe ride for the animals.

Transporting Animals

All animal transport vehicles should have a portable ramp for off-loading animals in case of emergencies. The floor of the vehicle should not be slippery to prevent the tripping of animals. Also, there should be adequate space in the vehicle for every animal to stand and move their heads. There should be a proper ventilation system.

All animal transport vehicles have proper ventilation system. True or False

Glossary

Broadcast: to announce some information to the general public with the means of television or radio

Ceremony: an official event that happens publicly

Commerce: related to money

Commercial: related to business

Depict: to express something in a drawing or picture

Elevated: lifted; raised high

English Channel: a channel that separates southern England from northern France

Equipped: necessary things or outfits required in any situation

Forecast: to say something in advance

Iceberg: a large floating mass of ice

Locomotive: a self-propelled engine that pulls a train

Mesopotamia: the area of land between the Tigris and Euphrates rivers

Participants: people who take part in a competition

Periscope: a long tube with mirrors at both ends that is used to look over the top of something, like the surface of the sea from a submarine

Propeller: equipment with blades that spin and help the ship or aircraft move forward

Rear: the back part of something

Rumbling: a heavy, continuous, rolling sound like thunder

Separate: to set apart something from others for a special purpose

Shipment: goods loaded in the ship

Shipwreck: the loss or destruction of a ship by storm or collision

Spy: a person who keeps a secret watch on others' actions

Sturdy: something physically strong

Supersonic: greater than the speed of sound

Answers

Page No. 9	Around 3500 BC in Mesopotamia
Page No. 11	Monsieur Sivrac
Page No. 13	Sylvester Howard Roper in 1869
Page No. 15	1908
Page No. 17	True
Page No. 19	USS Gerald R. Ford
Page No. 21	Trans-Siberian railway line
Page No. 23	Airbus A380
Page No. 25	First airship
Page No. 27	Hovercrafts
Page No. 29	Yuri Gagarin
Page No. 31	Joseph Bombardier
Page No. 33	To walk or move about
Page No. 35	Lester Wire
Page No. 37	48,000 kilometres (about 29,825 miles)
Page No. 39	Yes
Page No. 41	Robert T. Mawhinney
Page No. 43	True

INVENTIONS AND CREATIONS
WONDERS OF THE WORLD

Introduction

Some structures in the world are outstandingly magnificent. They leave visitors wonderstruck and are therefore known as "wonders of the world." These structures remind us of our past, as well as the natural world around us.

In ancient times, these magnificent structures were built using simple techniques and machines. These structures were the result of human intelligence, artistic skills and a huge labour force.

Colosseum

The Colosseum is a huge amphitheatre shaped like an oval. The construction of the Colosseum began around 2000 years ago, during the reign of Emperor Vespasian, and was completed by his son Titus. The name Colosseum comes from a large statue, or colossus, of the Roman Emperor Nero.

Exterior and Interior

The interior of the Colosseum had an acting area, a platform, and rows of seats. The emperor, men, and other important people sat near the acting area, while women and the poor occupied the upper rows. The Colosseum could accommodate up to 50,000 spectators at a time. The exterior was adorned with arches, windows and columns built in the Greek style.

Structure and Size

Early amphitheatres were built using wood. However, the Colosseum was built using iron and a high-quality marble known as travertine. The Colosseum is shaped like an ellipse, measuring 189 metres (615 feet) long and 156 metres (510 feet) wide. The height of the outer walls is about 47 metres (157 feet).

- The Colosseum had 80 entrances and around 240 arches.
- The Colosseum that we see today is just one-third of the original Colosseum.
- The last gladiatorial fights in the Colosseum took place in 435 AD.

The First Games

The Colosseum was built to amuse the Roman people. The first games held in the great amphitheatre lasted for around 100 days. The Romans mostly loved bullfights, fights between wild animals, theatre shows, and gladiator fights.

How many people could be seated in the Colosseum?

St. Peter's Basilica

Saint Peter's Basilica is one of the largest Christian churches in the world. It is named after Saint Peter, who was one of the twelve apostles of Jesus Christ. The Basilica is in the holy city of Vatican, and it was built between 1506 and 1626.

Largest Church of Its Time

Saint Peter's Basilica covers an area of 15,160 square meters (about 163,181 square feet) and can hold more than 60,000 people. It was the largest church in the world until 1989. The Basilica of our Lady of Peace of Yamoussoukro in the Republic of Côte d'Ivoire in West Africa became the largest church in 1989.

- The Vatican State is the smallest country in the world, with a population of about 800 people.
- Michelangelo, the great Italian Renaissance painter, sculptor and architect, contributed greatly to the architecture of the Basilica.
- Saint Peter was the first bishop of Rome.

The Art Work

Saint Peter's Basilica is one of the finest examples of Renaissance art. Many famous artists and sculptors of that time contributed to the creation of this artwork. Bernini's centrepiece is one of the most admired sculptures in the church.

Old St. Peter's Basilica

Old St. Peter's Basilica was built over St. Peter's grave. Constantine the Great, the first Christian Emperor of Rome, built it in the 4th century. The basilica that we see today was built to replace Old St. Peter's Basilica.

? Which church became the largest church in 1989?

Leaning Tower of Pisa

The Leaning Tower of Pisa is a bell tower located in the Italian city of Pisa. The tower was built around 800 years ago, in 1173 AD, and is famous all over the world for its leanness. The tower served as a bell tower for the Cathedral of Pisa.

The Lean

The Leaning Tower of Pisa began to lean towards the north after the construction of its first floor. The lean occurred because of the soft and sandy soil on which the tower was built. Today, the tower is leaning one millimetre every year towards the south. The lean made the top of the tower five metres (about 16 feet) away from its foundation.

Bells

The Leaning Tower has seven bells of different weights and sizes. The different shapes and sizes of bells help produce various musical sounds. The heaviest bell weighs about four tonnes, and the lightest bell weighs less than a tonne. All seven bells were hung at different times. The bells were used to call people to the cathedral for prayer.

The Structure

The Leaning Tower is made of marble, lime, and stones. It is about 55 metres (about 186 feet) in height and has eight floors. A 294-step spiral staircase is inside the tower, which leads to the bell hall.

? **How many feet away is the top of the Leaning Tower of Pisa from its foundation?**

- The German army used the tower to keep a watch on the enemy during World War II.
- In 1990, the bells of the Leaning Tower were silenced to prevent it from leaning further.
- In 1993, 650 tonnes of lead were hung from the north side of the building to try to stop the increasing lean.

Great Wall of China

The Great Wall of China is the longest man-made structure in the world. It is about 6,400 kilometres (about 3,977 miles) in length. Chinese rulers built smaller walls, which were later joined to make the Great Wall.

Material Used

The first wall was built using wood, stones, and rammed earth. The wall built during the Ming Dynasty was a stronger one. It was built using bricks and stones. Many parts of the wall were also constructed with tiles, lime, and stones. Lime mixed with sticky rice was used as cement to fill in between the bricks. This made the wall stronger.

Construction

The first part of the Great Wall was built during the rule of the first Chinese Emperor, Qin Shi Huangdi, in the 2nd century AD. The Great Wall that we see today was built during the rule of Emperor Ming in the late 15th century AD.

The Largest Structure

The Great Wall of China stretches over mountains, plains and valleys. The height and width of the wall are not the same everywhere. The Great Wall is wider and higher in the plains and lower and narrower in the mountains.

How long is the Great Wall of China?

- The Great Wall of China stretches from the eastern side to the western side of China.
- Emperor Ming hired about 300,000 peasants and prisoners who worked hard day and night to build the Great Wall.

Taj Mahal

The Taj Mahal is a mausoleum built by the fifth Mughal Emperor of India, Shah Jahan, in memory of his beloved wife, Arjumand Banu Begum, popularly known as Mumtaz Mahal. The Taj Mahal is located in the city of Agra, India.

The Structure

The construction of the Taj Mahal began in 1632 and was completed in 1653. The mausoleum consists of four identical facades, each containing a large central arch. The tomb was built on a raised, square-shaped platform with a minaret at each corner. The minarets are about 50 metres (164 feet) high. A large dome rises over the centre of the tomb, with four smaller domes surrounding it.

Workforce

The Taj Mahal is one of the greatest monuments of Islamic architecture. More than 20,000 workers and artisans worked for 22 years to build one of the most beautiful tombs in the world.

Facts

- The word Taj Mahal means "Crown Palace."
- Verses from the Holy Koran were inscribed outside the tomb.
- Workers and artisans from India, Iran, Turkey and Europe worked to build the Taj Mahal.

Materials Used

The Taj Mahal is one of the costliest tombs ever built. It is entirely made of white marble. Many semi-precious and rare stones were used to decorate the tomb. These stones, such as agate, turquoise, lapis lazuli, jade, coral, and bloodstone, were brought from China, Tibet, Sri Lanka, and Arabia.

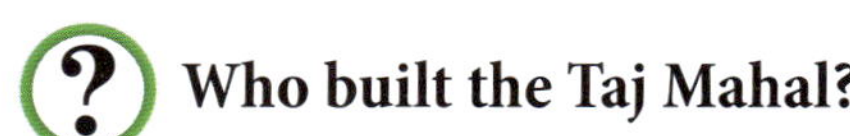

Who built the Taj Mahal?

Angkor Wat

Angkor Wat is the largest religious temple complex in the world. It was built in the 12th century AD for King Suryavarman II of the Khmer Empire. Angkor Wat is located in the city of Angkor, Cambodia.

The "Temple City"

Angkor Wat means the "temple city." It includes temples, palaces and buildings of the Khmer people. The temple of Angkor Wat has five carved towers that look like pyramids from a distance.

Longest Bas-Relief

Angkor Wat has the longest bas-relief carving in the world. The bas-relief is 800 metres (about 2,625 feet) long and 2 metres (about 7 feet) high. Bas-relief carvings are sculptures that project out slightly from the walls on which they are carved.

Materials Used

Angkor Wat was constructed using sandstone and laterite, a type of red soil formed from rock decay. Sandstone was transported from a nearby hill by river. Hundreds of workers, artisans, and slaves worked for 30 years to build this huge temple city.

- The national flag of Cambodia has a small picture of Angkor Wat.
- Angkor Wat also served as a tomb for Suryavarman II.
- Stories from great epics like the Ramayana and Mahabharata are also described in the bas-relief.
- Angkor Wat is a significant religious centre for Buddhists.

Where is the largest temple in the world?

Great Barrier Reef

The Great Barrier Reef is the largest coral reef in the world. It is a group of 3,000 reefs and 600 small islands. The reef stretches for 2,012 kilometres (about 1,250 miles) along the northeastern coast of Australia.

The Coral

Corals are marine animals. They belong to the family of sea anemones and jellyfish. They have a soft, cylindrical body known as a polyp. Coral polyps attach themselves to rocky bottoms in the sea and start multiplying. They build limestone shelters in which they live. These shelters join to form a large coral.

Barrier Reefs

Barrier reefs are reefs formed along the coastline. A wide, deep lagoon separates reefs from the shore. Barrier reefs are called so because they act as a barrier between the ocean and shore.

Marine Life

The Great Barrier Reef is home to many species of sea animals and birds. Many endangered species of animals, such as whales, dolphins and sea turtles, are found here. It is also home to 29 species of seabirds, and 9,000 species of marine life.

Facts

- The Great Barrier Reef Marine Park is larger than the U.K. and Ireland combined.
- The Great Barrier Reef is the only living natural group visible from Earth's orbit.

How long is the Great Barrier Reef?

Machu Picchu

Machu Picchu was an ancient city of the Incas built on the top of a mountain in Peru, South America. The building was constructed between 1460 and 1470 under the direction of Pachacuti Inca Yupanqui, who was the Incan King at the time. The city was probably built as a royal estate and religious retreat for the king. Machu Picchu was known as the "lost city" until 1911, when its ruins were discovered by an archaeologist.

People

Farming was the primary occupation of the Incans. They cultivated two significant crops: potatoes and maize. The men mainly tended to the farms and fields, while women stayed home to weave, create pottery, and engage in handicrafts.

The City

The city of Machu Picchu had temples, buildings, storage buildings, parks, and courtyards. Houses were built in groups of ten with a common courtyard.

Population

Around 1200 people lived in the city of Machu Picchu. It was inhabited by metalworkers, officials and servants. There were more women and children than men.

The End

After 62 years of existence, life at Machu Picchu ended. Around 50 percent of the population died of smallpox. The rest of the population was killed when Spanish explorers plundered Machu Picchu in 1533.

- Incans joined building blocks without using cement.
- Houses in the city of Machu Picchu did not have roofs.
- Machu Picchu was the royal residence of the Inca kings.

What was Machu Picchu known as till 1911?

Grand Canyon

The Grand Canyon is one of the natural wonders of the world. It is a deep, wide, and steep-walled canyon formed by the Colorado River. It includes many canyons and is located in Arizona, United States. The first recorded exploration of the Grand Canyon was by Spanish explorer Garcia Lopez de Cardenas in 1540.

Colorado River

The Colorado River is 2,330 kilometres (about 1450 miles) long and flows from the Rocky Mountains. The Colorado River took six million years to form the Grand Canyon. The river looks red in colour because of the volcanic remains and deposits.

Colourful Landscapes

The Grand Canyon is one of the most beautiful canyons in the world. It is famous for its colourful landscapes.

The Two Rims

The Grand Canyon has two rims: the North Rim and the South Rim. The Kaibab Plateau forms the North Rim, while the Coconino Plateau forms the South Rim. The North Rim is about 365 metres (1200 feet) higher than the South Rim.

Facts

- In the Grand Canyon, around 50 different kinds of reptiles and 300 species of birds are found.
- The oldest fossils found here are around 12,000 years old.
- The Grand Canyon is spread across three of North America's four deserts.

How long is the Colorado River?

Pyramid at Chichén Itzá

The ancient Mayan people built the Pyramid of Chichén Itzá. They used it as a temple. The pyramid is known as "El Castillo." "El Castillo" in Spanish means "the castle." It was built between 550 AD and 800 AD in Mexico.

Structure

The pyramid is 23 metres (about 75 feet) high with a square base. The four sides of the base have nine platforms. On these nine platforms, there are four staircases. Each staircase has 91 steps. By adding all the steps together, along with the one at the top of the temple, there are 365 steps. Each step represents a day of the solar year, which means the staircase served as a calendar.

Village Life

Mayan people had small families. They lived together in tiny villages. Their huts were made of interwoven wooden poles and thatched roofs. They used their huts only for sleeping. Cooking was done outside their huts in a common open area.

The City of Chichén Itzá

Chichén Itzá means "at the mouth of the well of the Itzá." The city of Chichén Itzá was built near wells. As water was scarce in that area, people settled near wells which provided water for agriculture and drinking purposes.

Facts

- The Mayan number system included zero.
- The four staircases represent the four cycles of life: infanthood, childhood, adulthood, and old age.
- El Castillo was built on another temple.

? **How many steps does El Castillo have?**

Christ the Redeemer

Christ the Redeemer is a statue of Jesus Christ. It is one of the biggest statues in the world. It is situated on the top of Corcovado Mountain in Rio de Janeiro, the former capital of Brazil. The construction of the statue began in 1922 and was completed in 1931.

The Statue

The statue of Christ the Redeemer was built to celebrate Brazil's one hundred years of freedom from Portuguese rule. The statue is 39 metres (about 130 feet) high and can be seen from any part of Rio de Janeiro. The open arms of Christ are 30 metres (about 98 feet) long from one fingertip to another. Each arm weighs 57 tonnes.

The Structure

Christ the Redeemer is one of the best monuments ever built in the world. It is made of reinforced concrete and soapstone so that it can remain firmly seated on the ground even in bad weather. The statue weighs about 1,145 tonnes.

The Design

Carlos Oswaldo created the initial design for the statue. It showed Christ holding a globe in one hand and a cross in another. However, it was rejected. Later, a Brazilian designer, Heitor da Silva Costa, designed the present statue. His design showed Christ with wide-open arms, ready to embrace people.

Where is the statue of Christ the Redeemer located?

Facts

- Christ the Redeemer was declared a Catholic sanctuary in 2006 by the Roman Catholic Church.
- The head of Christ was made by joining 50 pieces.
- The monument was originally green, but now it looks grey due to pollution.
- The statue looks like a cross.

Great Pyramid of Giza

The Great Pyramid of Giza is the largest of all the pyramids ever built. It was built between 2600 and 2500 BC in Egypt. The Great Pyramid is the tomb of an Egyptian king, Khufu, and is also known as the Pyramid of Khufu. It is the only surviving ancient wonder of the world.

Facts

- Timber sleds were used to transport stone blocks from one place to another.
- Around 100,000 workers worked to build the Great Pyramid of Giza.
- Egyptians buried the Pharaoh after making his mummy.

The Structure

It took nearly 20 years to build the Great Pyramid. It was built with the help of 2 million stone blocks. Each stone block weighs more than 2 tonnes. In total, the Great Pyramid weighs about 6 million tonnes.

Three Chambers

The Great Pyramid was divided into three chambers. The first chamber was known as the King's chamber, in which the body of Pharaoh Khufu was buried. The second chamber was known as the Queen's chamber, where all the necessary things like food and jewels were kept. The third chamber was known as the underground chamber, which might have been built to fool robbers.

Tallest Structure of its Time

For more than 43,000 years, the Great Pyramid remained the tallest structure on earth. It was the tallest until 1889, when the Eiffel Tower was built. The Eiffel Tower is 324 metres (about 1,063 feet) high. The Great Pyramid was 147 metres (about 482 feet) high when it was built and is now only 138 metres (about 453 feet) high.

The Great Pyramid of Giza is the tomb of ________.

Petra

Petra is an ancient city built from rocks. In Greek, the word petra means "rock." The city is famous for its beautiful buildings, which were carved from red sandstone hills. Petra was built between 100 BC and 100 AD and is located in southwestern Jordan.

Trade City

Petra was the capital city of an Arab tribe called the Nabataeans. Nabataeans were nomads who lived around 2,000 years ago. Petra became an important trading centre when they started trading. Traders from China, India, southern Arabia, Egypt, Syria, Greece, and Rome crossed Petra. They traded in textiles, incense, silk, and spices.

Carving a Tomb

The city of Petra has hundreds of tombs and buildings. Skilled stonemasons, guided by a master artisan, carved the stone from top to bottom.

Theme and Design

Nabataeans were very much inspired by the designs of East and West. They carved vines, flowers, animals, and people. A 42-metre (about 138 feet)-high temple in front of the El-Deir Monastery is the best example of the Nabataea designs.

- Nabataeans built a theatre like what the Greeks and Romans built, with sitting space for 4,000 people.
- Petra's water supply system supplied 12 million gallons of water everyday, enough for 100,000 Americans.
- Petra was first discovered by a Swiss traveler, Johann L. Burckhardt.

Hagia Sophia

The Hagia Sophia is a former church and mosque and is now a museum of Byzantine art. It is located in Istanbul, Turkey. The Hagia Sophia was built as a church by the Byzantine Emperor Justinian I in 537 AD. The church was converted into a mosque in 1453, when Constantinople was conquered by the Ottoman Turks. In 1935, it was turned into the Ayasofya Museum by the Turkish President, Kemal Atatürk.

The Dome

The Hagia Sophia is one of the finest works of Byzantine architecture. It is famous all over the world for its huge dome. It is 31 metres (about 102 feet) in diameter and 56 metres (184 feet) high, with 40 windows. The windows illuminate the hall. Around 10,000 workers worked on the construction of the Hagia Sophia.

The Decorations

The interior of the Hagia Sophia was beautifully decorated. Mosaic paintings were the most popular of the various methods used in the cathedral. They were made by using stone, glass and other materials over a gold background. The most famous of all paintings was of Jesus Christ sitting between Emperor Constantine and Justinian.

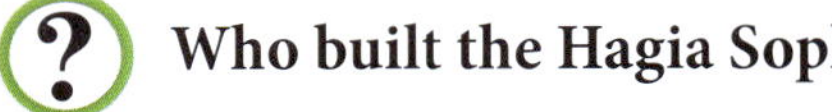

Who built the Hagia Sophia?

- The emperor appointed around 600 people to serve the great church.
- Hagia Sophia is a Greek word that means "Holy Wisdom of Christ."
- Hagia Sophia was built in less than six years.

Victoria Falls

Victoria Falls is one of the greatest and most beautiful waterfalls in the world. It lies on the Zambezi River, which flows from the border of two south-central African countries, Zambia and Zimbabwe.

Flying Water

Victoria Falls has the largest falling water sheet in the world. Every minute, Victoria Falls tumbles 142 billion gallons of water deep into the valley. The falling water thunders and its drizzle flies up to a height of 304 metres (about 997 feet). When sunlight falls on the drizzles, it forms beautiful rainbows.

Widest in the World

Victoria Falls is around 1.6 kilometres (about 1 mile) wide and more than 108 metres (about 354 feet) deep. It is twice as wide and deep as Niagara Falls.

- In the local African language, Victoria Falls is known as Mosi-oa-Tunya, which means "the smoke that thunders."
- Livingstone is a city near Victoria Falls, named after David Livingstone.
- Archaeologists believe that Victoria Falls was the "birthplace of mankind."

Discovery of the Falls

British explorer David Livingstone discovered Victoria Falls in 1855 and named it after Queen Victoria of Great Britain.

Who discovered Victoria Falls?

Burj Khalifa

Burj Khalifa is the tallest skyscraper in the world. This tallest man-made freestanding structure is in Dubai, United Arab Emirates. Initially, the soaring building was called Burj Dubai but was renamed after the president of the UAE and ruler of Abu Dhabi, Sheikh Khalifa bin Zayed Al Nahyan.

World's Grandest

Burj Khalifa has the world's highest observation deck on the 124th floor, the highest mosque on the 158th floor, the tallest lift service, and the highest occupied floor. The skyscraper is even taller than Taipei 101, the previous record holder for the tallest building. Taipei 101 was 509 metres (1,671 feet) tall.

Construction

The construction of Burj Khalifa began on September 21, 2004. More than 45,000 cubic metres (58,900 cubic yards) of concrete were used for the construction of the foundation of Burj Khalifa.

- The world's tallest performing fountain, the Dubai Fountain, lies at the bottom of the Burj Khalifa.
- The total weight of aluminium used in the construction of Burj Khalifa is equal to that of five A-380 aircraft.
- Burj Khalifa became operational for the public on January 4, 2010.

Great Stature

Burj Khalifa is 828 metres (2,716 feet) tall and has around 200 floors, of which 163 are for living purposes. The building has 1044 luxury apartments, office floors, the Armani Hotel, and residences. Burj Khalifa is so tall that its spire can be seen 95 kilometres (60 miles) away.

How tall is Burj Khalifa?

Stonehenge

Stonehenge, near Salisbury in Wiltshire, in southern England, is one of the oldest and most wonderful ancient structures. It was built around 5,000 years ago. The builders of this awe-inspiring structure and the purpose of its construction are still cloaked in mystery.

Trilithons

A trilithon is a structure of two stones placed vertically on the ground that are supported by a third stone placed horizontally over them. Five trilithons, each weighing 50 tonnes, were arranged from smaller to bigger in the shape of a horseshoe inside Stonehenge.

Inner Stone Circle

Construction of Stonehenge began as a round earthen bank and ditch with wooden posts. Later, in 2600 BC, the wooden posts were replaced by 80 bluestones. Each bluestone weighed up to four tonnes. These stones were believed to have been brought from the Preseli Mountains, situated 386 kilometres (240 miles) away in Wales. They formed the Inner Stone Circle of Stonehenge.

Outer Stone Circle

A few years later, 'Sarsen' stones were brought from Marlborough Towns, 30 kilometres (20 miles) north of Stonehenge. These giant sandstone slabs were about 2.4 metres (8 feet) wide, 1.5 metres (5 feet) thick, and 7.6 metres (25 feet) long. Each of the slabs weighed about 20 to 30 tonnes. About 30 sarsen stones were used to build the outer circle.

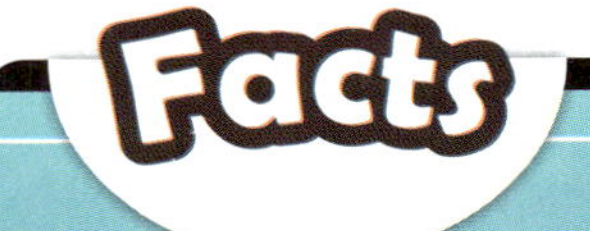

- In Greek, trilithon means 'three stones'.
- Many researchers believe that Stonehenge was an astronomical site, while others believe it was a place of worship.
- According to research, it probably took about 20 million hours to construct Stonehenge.

How many trilithons were set in Stonehenge?

Moai

Moai are large, monolithic, upright human-like statues on Easter Island, Chile. They were carved from volcanic rock between 1250 and 1500 AD by the Polynesian colonisers.

Facts

- Moai were also called the 'Easter Island Heads'.
- A total of 887 statues were discovered in a complete or partially complete state on Easter Island.
- The largest finished moai is more than 9.14 metres (30 feet) tall, and the smallest is 1.80 metres (6 feet) tall.

What were Moai?

Almost all the Moai statues were carved in male form. The statues have large heads with angular faces, heavy eyebrows, large eye sockets, elongated noses and ears, and thin lips placed on a smaller torso. According to many scholars, the moai were crafted in honour of deities, ancestors, chiefs, or other extremely important people.

How were they carved?

Archaeologists discovered most of the Moai statues while excavating the volcanic crater of Rano Raraku. The moai were carved into the walls of the crater. First, the outline of the shape was marked with the help of a keel. Once the carving of the front of the statue was complete, the statue was removed from the wall very carefully and carried down the slope of the crater. Then the back of the statue was carved.

Ahu Akivi

Ahu is a flat mound on which moai were placed. Ahu Akivi is a site where seven almost identical moai were placed facing the ocean. This is the only site where this was done, as other moai were erected to face the island.

What is Rano Raraku?

Glossary

Ancestor: somebody who is related to you and lived a long time ago

Ancient: very old

Archaeologist: a person who studies ancient life by examining objects and tools of the past.

Astronomical: related to the study of stars and planets

Byzantine art: art of the Byzantine era or the Eastern Roman Empire

Cambodia: a country in Southeast Asia

Carved: to cut a statue by cutting it from stone

Crater: a large and deep pit

Elongated: longer and narrower

Embrace: to clasp in the arms

Explorer: a person who travels to unknown or unfamiliar places

Illuminate: to make a place bright with light.

Landscape: a picture of natural, inland scenery, such as woodland or mountains

Monolith: any piece of sculpture carved out of a single large block or piece of stone

Mosaic: a design made from different coloured stones

Mosque: a place of worship for Muslims

Nomad: a person who moves from place to place and does not have a Permanent home.

Pharaoh: an Egyptian king

Plunder: to rob or raid a place by force.

Reign: to rule as a king or queen over a country

Renaissance: an art movement in Europe between the 14th and 17th centuries

Scarce: not enough in supply

Skyscraper: a very tall building

Verses: a sequence of words arranged in poetic form

Answers

Page No. 51	50,000
Page No. 53	The Basilica of our Lady of Peace of Yamoussoukro
Page No. 55	16 feet
Page No. 57	6,400 kilometers (about 3,977 miles)
Page No. 59	Emperor Shah Jahan
Page No. 61	Cambodia
Page No. 63	2,012 kilometres (1,250 miles)
Page No. 65	Lost city
Page No. 67	2,330 kilometres (about 1,450 miles)
Page No. 69	365
Page No. 71	Rio de Janeiro, Brazil
Page No. 73	King Khufu
Page No. 75	True
Page No. 77	Emperor Justinian I
Page No. 79	David Livingstone
Page No. 81	828 metres (2,716 feet) tall
Page No. 83	Five
Page No. 85	A volcanic crater